This Ladybird book
belongs to

_____

All Ladybird books are available at most bookshops,
supermarkets and newsagents, or can be ordered direct from:

Ladybird Postal Sales
PO Box 133 Paignton TQ3 2YP England
Telephone: (+44) 01803 554761
Fax: (+44) 01803 663394

A catalogue record for this book is available
from the British Library

Published by Ladybird Books Ltd
A subsidiary of the Penguin Group
A Pearson Company
© LADYBIRD BOOKS LTD MCMXCVIII

LADYBIRD and the device of a Ladybird are trademarks of
Ladybird Books Ltd Loughborough Leicestershire UK

Woof! Woof!
first picture
word book

illustrated by **Angie Sage**

Ladybird

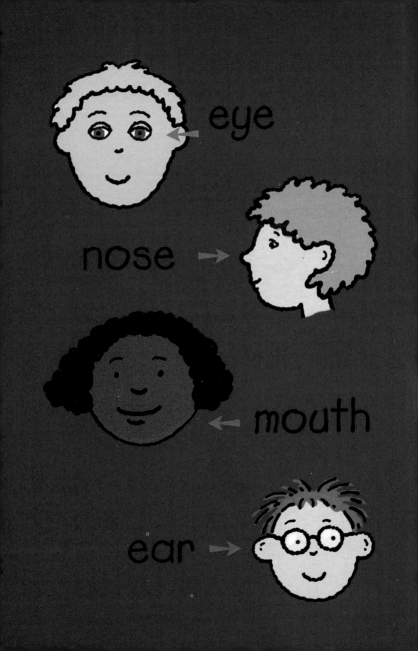

eye

nose →

← mouth

ear →

← hair

tongue →

eyebrow

teeth →

socks

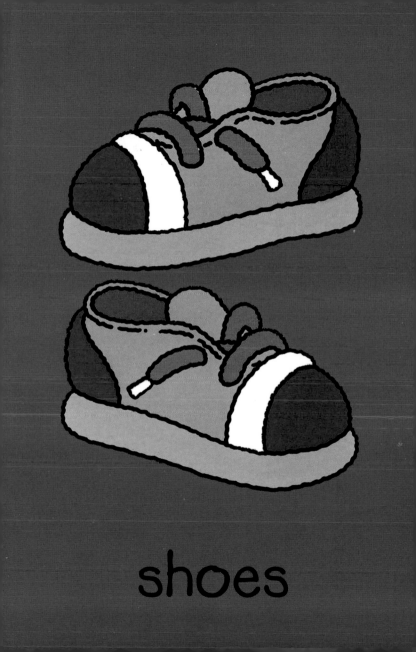

shoes

sweater

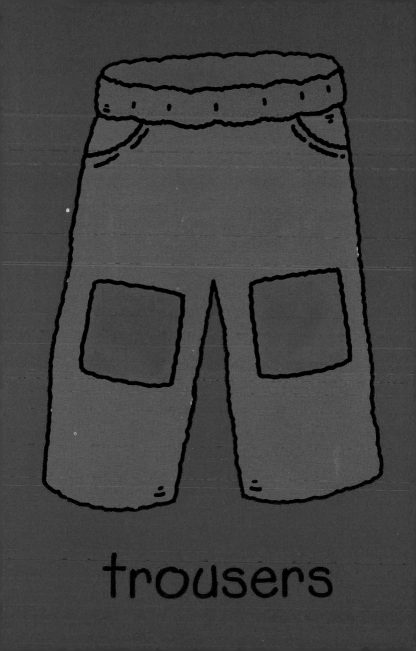

trousers

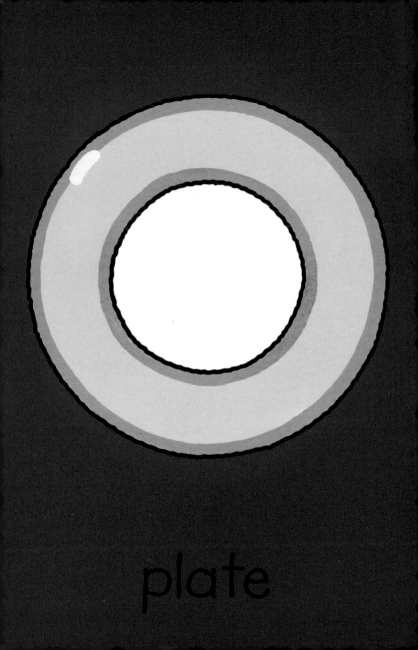

plate

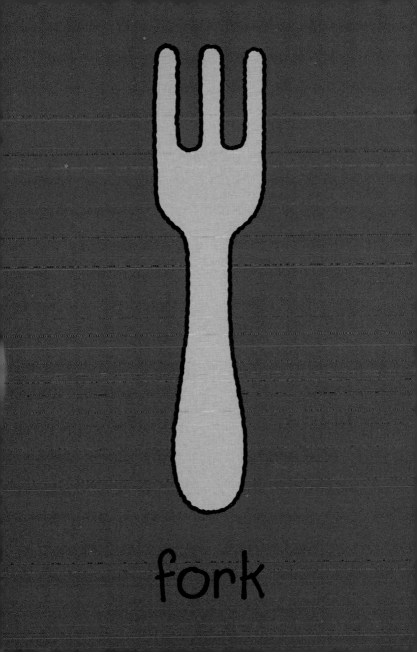

fork

apple

juice

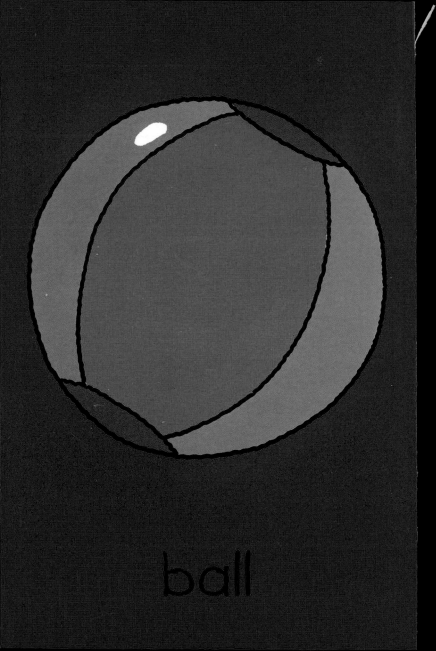

ball

doll

book

Brring! Brring!

phone

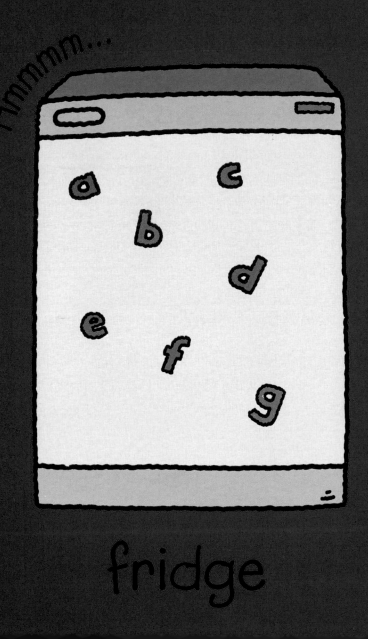

Swosh! Swosh!

washing machine

television

Vooom! Vooom!

vacuum cleaner

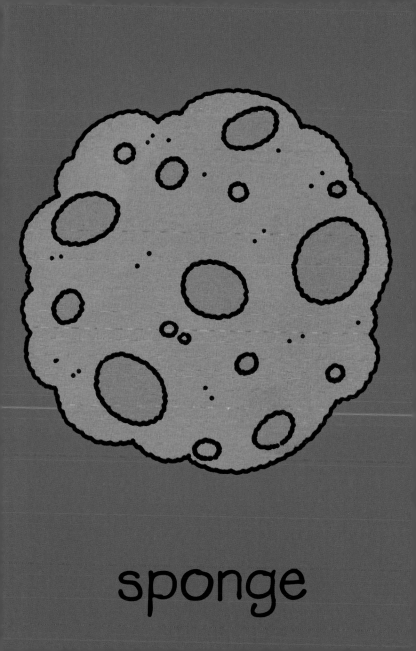

sponge

pyjamas

slippers